TED

· ShoeBoxx SpyBot ·

· Phat Tyre ·

· Scetti da Strainer ·

· Hose-Nose ·

· Viking Boch ·

BUCKY AND STU vs. THE MIKANIKAL MAN

story and art by **Cornelius Van Wright**

NANCY PAULSEN BOOKS ✺ AN IMPRINT OF PENGUIN GROUP (USA)

To En-Wei

NANCY PAULSEN BOOKS
Published by the Penguin Group
Penguin Group (USA) LLC
375 Hudson Street, New York, NY 10014

USA | Canada | UK | Ireland | Australia
New Zealand | India | South Africa | China
penguin.com
A Penguin Random House Company

Library of Congress Cataloging-in-Publication Data is available upon request.

Manufactured in China by South China Printing Co. Ltd.
ISBN 978-0-399-16427-9
1 3 5 7 9 10 8 6 4 2

Design by Ryan Thomann. Text set in Kosmik.
The art was done in watercolors and pencil on illustration board.

BUCKY AND STU spent the morning preparing the backyard for the great battle ahead.

They examined the pictures of the most wanted bad guys on the planet.

It's up to them to stop Phat Tyre
and his crew of baddies, for they are
the protectors of their **hometown**,

their **planet**

and their **favorite TV show.**

Bucky and Stu shout their favorite battle cry:

"WONK 'EM TIME!"

Down goes
Baddie BOXMAN!

Combining their powers,
Bucky and Stu topple TrashMan!

OH NO!

Stu is captured
by the sneaky
Hose-Nose!

In the nick of time, Bucky
pushes Hose-Nose's snout button

and Stu breaks free!

Just as our heroes get ready to face the main villain, Phat Tyre, Stu is stopped in his tracks by . . .

GURGLE

"Hey, you can't leave now.
We have to defeat Phat Tyre."

"Stu hungry. Stu needs snack . . . "

Fortunately, Stu's mom has a big lunch waiting for the boys.
Stu eats 6 tacos, 3 burritos, 2 hot dogs and a salad.
Bucky has a taco.

"Where do you put it all?"

AFTER LUNCH . . .

"I have a secret,"
Bucky whispers to Stu.

"Fighting pretend bad guys is fun, but what if we could battle a real, live nemesis?" he asks.

"What's a *nemesis?*"

At the edge of town, Bucky shows Stu a mysteriously covered . . . **something.**

"Uncle Ernie and I have been building this for a while," Bucky tells Stu.

FX086 SUPERCOMPUTER
(SLIGHTLY DAMAGED)

UNCLE ERNIE'S CYCLE FENDERS

"All he needs now is a Bio-Mechanical Nuclear Power Pac!" says Bucky.

"Yes, a Nuclear Power Pac!" says Stu.

PHILCO AMAZING CRT

It starts to rain, so the boys cover the Mikanikal Man and head for home.

"Let's find a Power Pac tomorrow," says Stu.

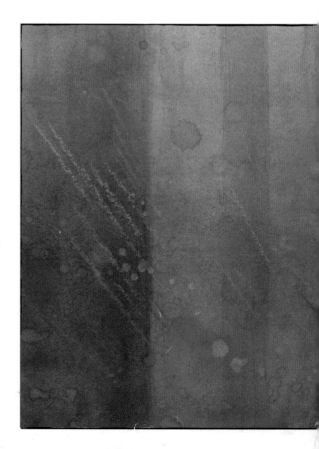

Bucky sleeps over at Stu's house. The lightning and thunder put on quite a show.

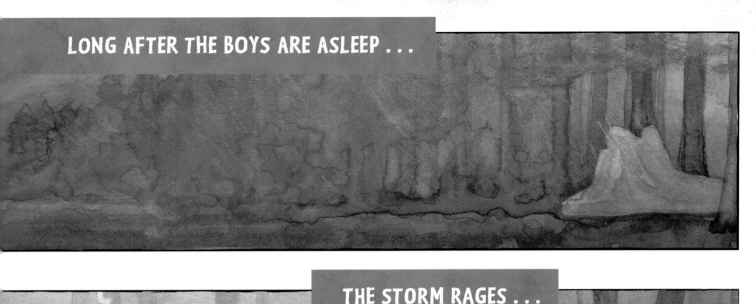

LONG AFTER THE BOYS ARE ASLEEP . . .

THE STORM RAGES . . .

In the morning, Bucky and Stu head back to the Mikanikal Man, but when they arrive . . .

"He's gone! Where is he?"

They search high and low.

But they can't find him anywhere.

Somebody stole the Mikanikal Man.

"MOMMA!"

"Wait a minute! We've pledged to protect our town. Protect our planet—"

"And our favorite TV show."

"We have to stop the Mikanikal Man from reaching town. That means it's . . ."

"WONK 'EM TIME!"

With great bravery, Bucky and Stu attack the Mikanikal Man . . .

But to no avail.

Is this
THE END
for our fearless heroes?

The end of
their town?

Their planet?

Their favorite
TV show?

BUT THEN . . .
"Stu, your timing is impeccable!"
GURGLE!
"That's not me!"
GURGLE!

The Mikanikal Man gently releases Bucky and Stu.

The boys feel bad for the Mikanikal Man.

"I know how you feel."

"THAT'S IT!
Wait right here, Mikanikal Man."

Bucky and Stu raid Uncle Ernie's garage
and bring back batteries, tubes and anything
they can find to feed Mikanikal Man.

"Boy, can he
put it away!"

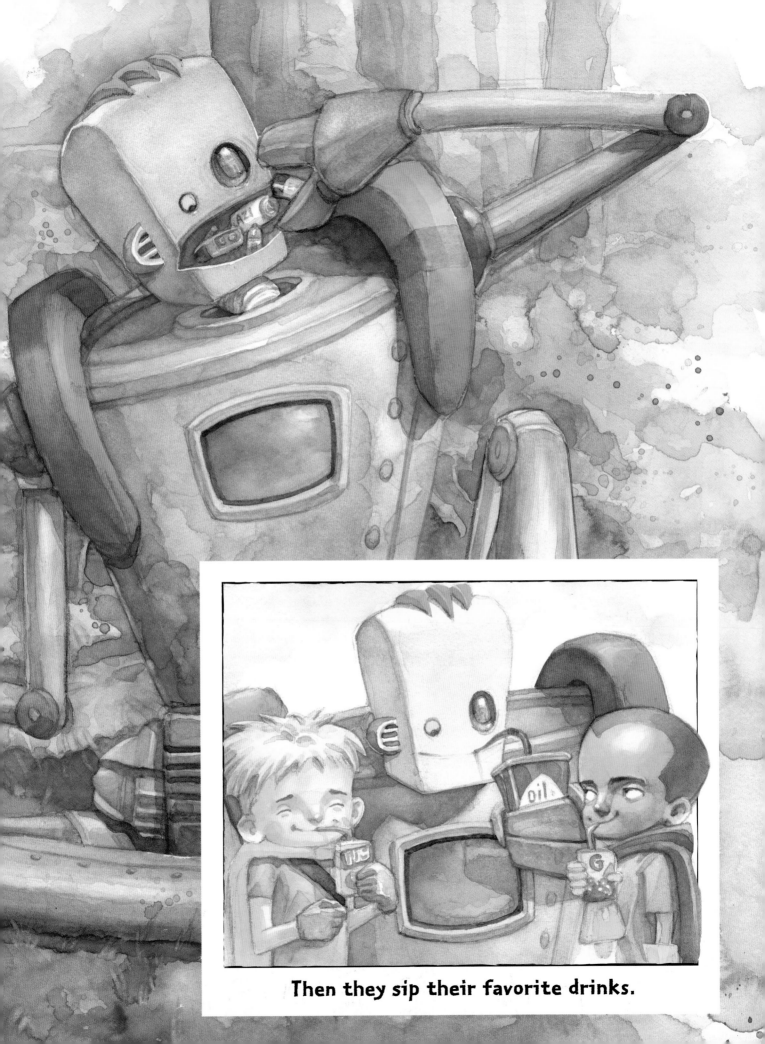

Then they sip their favorite drinks.

The Mikanikal Man is so happy, he gives
Bucky and Stu a ride they will always remember!